Philip's Little Sister

Words by Ellen Benson

Pictures by Rachael Davis

 CHILDRENS PRESS, CHICAGO

Copyright© 1979 by Regensteiner Publishing Enterprises, Inc.
All rights reserved. Published simultaneously in Canada.
Printed in the United States of America.

1 2 3 4 5 6 7 8 9 10 11 12 R 85 84 83 82 81 80 79

Library of Congress Cataloging in Publication Data

Benson, Ellen.
  Philip's little sister.

  SUMMARY: When Philip's bicycle is stolen, he
discovers his younger sister isn't quite the pest
he thought.
  [1. Brothers and sisters—Fiction] I. Davis,
Rachael. II. Title.
PZ7.B4472Ph   [E]   78-12627
ISBN 0-516-02023-4

Philip's Little Sister

"Calm down, Lynn," said her mother. "Stop crying and tell me what it is. But before you do, please close the door. We have enough mosquitoes in the house already."

"It's that rotten Philip," Lynn said, sobbing. "I was playing with the skateboard with Annie, and Philip came and took it away."

"Well," said Mrs. Tucker, her arms around her daughter, "it is his week to use the skateboard. We didn't think we had to buy two, and so you have to share it."

"But he didn't want to use it until he saw that I was having a good time," Lynn said.

"That's how Philip is sometimes. But you do the same thing," Mrs. Tucker pointed out. "Sometimes when it's your week and he's watching TV, you change the channel just so he can't see his favorite programs."

"I don't," said Lynn, although she knew she did. "But he does it more than I do. And he always thinks he's so *big*! Just because he's older than I am."

Mrs. Tucker nodded. "The difference between nine and seven can be *e-nor-mous* sometimes," she said.

Lynn really had to put up with a lot from her brother. In school she wasn't Lynn, but Philip's little sister. If Lynn hadn't done good work one day, the teacher would say, "Now Lynn, I'm surprised. Philip would have done much better."

Other people often compared them too. One of her grandmothers would say, "But Lynn, Philip never did that." Or, "Lynn, Philip liked to sit on my lap." Or, "Lynn, Philip used to like to come over to our house for a few days."

And then there were the hand-me-downs. Philip's first bicycle was a brand new one. A short time ago Philip's old bicycle had become Lynn's "new" one when he got a blue five-speed bike with red stripes.

Many of Lynn's toys and books had belonged to Philip.

And even though she was a girl, Lynn often wore some of Philip's clothing. When he outgrew his yellow raincoat and winter jacket, they were passed down to Lynn.

Lynn knew she really couldn't blame Philip for these things. But she could blame him for calling her "Cry baby," or just plain "Baby," or "Flynn" instead of her real name. And she could blame him for making fun of her when he was with his friends, and telling them how useless she was.

Of course she couldn't run as fast or jump as far as he could. She couldn't throw or catch a ball as well. Or swim. It didn't make any difference to him that she was two years younger. "Let's face it, Flynn," he would say. "You're just not much good for anything."

One morning Mrs. Tucker sent Philip to Riley's grocery store to pick up some hamburger rolls. The store was nearby. He could bicycle over in just a few minutes, park his bike outside Riley's, and go in. The trip wouldn't take long.

Of course Philip wouldn't let Lynn go with him. Off he rode on his new bicycle.

Lynn decided to ride too. She didn't have any special place to go. When she reached a corner, she saw her brother's bike speeding by. She knew it was his right away by the red stripes and the little light on the handlebars. But Philip wasn't on it. A much bigger boy was.

Lynn made up her mind. She would try to follow him. She couldn't keep up with him, but she could keep him in sight. The boy looked over his shoulder a few times, but he didn't notice a seven-year-old girl well behind him. Luckily for Lynn, the boy didn't go very far. She saw him turn down a long street with many trees on it and many children playing. Then she couldn't see him any more.

Lynn asked some of the children whether they had seen him. One girl about her own age told her that the bike and its rider had gone down a certain driveway. The girl said the boy's name was Butch Metzger. He had driven the bike into his garage, closed the door, and gone into his house. Lynn spotted the house number and rode home as fast as she could.

In the living room Philip was crying. Mrs. Tucker, sitting in a chair, had her arms around him. She was trying to comfort him.

"You don't have to tell me what happened," Lynn said. "Somebody stole Philip's bike. Right?"

"How did you know?" her mother asked.

Lynn quickly explained. Philip stopped crying and listened. "It's in a garage at 1220 Oak Street. The boy's name is Butch Metzger," she ended her story.

Mrs. Tucker ran to the telephone and
called the police. Then they drove over to
1220 Oak Street.

A police car was already there. One of the
policemen was looking in the garage through a
little window at the side. He was nodding his
head. The other policeman was knocking on
the front door.

"Lynn," Philip said as they got out of the car, "I'm . . . I'm sorry. I won't ever say anything bad about you again. We'll be friends. Forever."

Lynn smiled happily. So did Mrs. Tucker.